MW00581044

THE PUMPKIN MAN VS THE BOOGIE MAN

Written and Created by
Joe "The Gamer" Petraro
Pictures by Joe Petraro and Anne Petraro

Copyright © 2020 Joe "The Gamer" Petraro
All rights reserved
First Edition

Fulton Books, Inc.
Meadville, PA

Published by Fulton Books 2020

ISBN 978-1-64654-187-4 (paperback)
ISBN 978-1-64654-478-3 (digital)

Printed in the United States of America

Dedication

For Mrs. Drummy and Sensei Steven.

Once upon a time, Pumpkin-man and Pumpkinwoman were walking their dog.

The Boogie Man saw them and got very jealous. The Boogie Man did not like to see anyone happy.

4

No one could see the Boogie Man. He was invisible during the day. He watched Pumpkinman's family all day. The Boogie Man didn't like pumpkins and certainly hated love.

The Boogie Man planned to scare Pumpkinman at 3:00 a.m. He wanted to ruin everyone's happiness.

Pumpkinwoman has always
been afraid of the Boogie Man
at night. Pumpkinman always
protects her.

Pumpkinwoman and Pumpkin-man had a great evening at home. They ate dinner and decorated pumpkins.

As Pumpkinman and Pump-
kinwoman were sleeping, the
Boogie Man started making
loud noises at 3:00 a.m.

Buddy, the Pumpkindog, woke up Pumpkinman. Pumpkinman was *mad!* Pumpkinman said to the Boogie Man, "Meet me at the dojo now. We will handle this the right way!"

The Boogie Man took all their pumpkins and Buddy and put them in cages.

"If I win, I will keep them all! No one will be happy again!" said the Boogie Man.

"If I win, you will go away forever! Everyone will be happy. Pumpkins will be everywhere, and you will disappear," said Pumpkinman.

Pumpkinwoman followed them to the dojo, crying and terrified.

Pumpkinman was worried and remembered what Sensei always told him. Believe in yourself and never give up! The Boogie Man kept punching and kicking Pumpkinman, but he did "hot floor," some fakes, and finally—punch, two kicks, and a take-down!

"Kiai! Pumpkinman won!" Pumpkinwoman yelled. "Great take-down, Pumpkinman!"

Buddy and all the pumpkins were free! Happiness was all over!

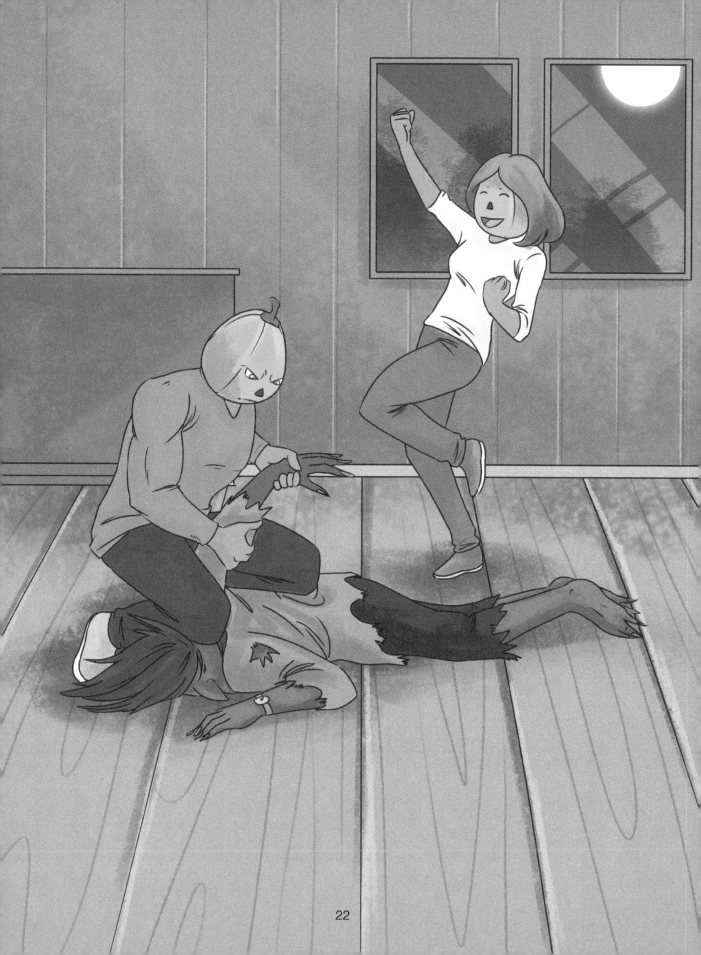

The Boogie Man disappeared, never to be seen again!

Everyone was so happy!

As the family hugged and embraced, they noticed Joe the Cub Scout outside selling popcorn. The Pumpkin King family bought so much popcorn, and Joe celebrated with them! It was already early morning now, and everyone relaxed.

The End

About the Author

Joe the Gamer resides in New York with his parents Ozzie and Anne and their two dogs, Buddy and Penny. Joe is a very creative child who enjoys creating episodes on his YouTube channel, writing fictional stories, and training for karate. Joe is a funny kid who loves spending time with his family and friends.